This story is dedicated to my children, Matilda and Hamish Jarvis, for it was their fascination of—and their fantastically wild theories about—what these strange deep sea sounds could possibly be, that gave me the idea for this story.

I love you, kiddos!

x
Jasmine, October 2020

I sat in the waiting room of the psychiatrist's office, jigging my left leg and with both my hands gripping the armrests. Across from me in this small waiting room sits another man... well, it wants you to think it is a man, but I know better. I see through its clever disguise. I catch it staring at me. To anyone else, they see a human, but to me I see one of *them*.

They are after me, trying to stop me, like they did to the others before me. My grip tightens on the armrests and I feel a prickling sensation run over my scalp. I break from the creature's threatening stare, and I look over at the receptionist behind the counter. She is slowly typing out session notes and is oblivious to what is in the room with her. I feel like I am choking—a scream caught in my throat. My heart is pounding so hard I am convinced that if I can't get out of here now, my heart will explode and like the others before me, I will drop dead right here in this cursed office.

"Mr Angus Ford?" My attention snaps to the figure standing in the doorway to one of the consultation rooms. Psychiatrist Doctor Gerald Meyers—I had been ordered by the judge to see him as part of my current legal "issue." I am not at fault though, I swear! I just need someone to take me seriously before it is too late for us all. I steady my nerves and stand up from the seat. I feel those bulbous black eyes burning into me as I force myself to move towards the doctor who is patiently waiting for me in the doorway to his office. As I pass the "man" sitting there, I look straight at him to see a menacing sneer distort its hellish features. Then, just as quickly, its face returned to human form while it glared at me. I clenched my fists to stop myself from punching it—that is what got me here in the first place. Well, not punching, I stabbed the last one, but I digress.

Doctor Meyers was an old man—bald, save for a few white wispy strands of hair peppered around his ears. His eyebrows were bushy too, like caterpillars (I notice these things as I spiral further down into this madness). Liver spots dotted across his old, pale white skin; wearing a fancy suit, he looked every inch a credible doctor (how I perceived a credible doctor to look), and human. My heart slowed down and the prickling in my scalp ceased. I swallowed the scream, and finally I could breathe again. Doctor Meyers showed me to the daybed and insisted I lie down and make myself comfortable. As I settled into the soft cushions, he placed a glass of water on the stand beside me and he took his place in a big leather armchair—retrieving his notebook and pen from one armrest.

"Mr Ford, I am Doctor Meyers and I am so glad we can meet and talk today. Do you mind if I call you Angus?" I let out a sigh and nodded. "Yes, Angus is fine." "Good, good. Now I understand you are having some"—he flicked through a manila folder containing the notes from my lawyer and the pending court case—"hallucinations. Can you tell me about these hallucinations you have been having, and for how long have you been seeing"—he referred to the case notes again—"fishlike people, aliens, and demonic forces, for?" He looked at me with old, watery grey eyes, his pen poised above the paper, ready to start taking my notes.

I let my head sink back into the cushions, bringing my hands up to my face. I pushed the palms of my hands hard into my eyes to bring about the "fireworks." I realised that I was now trembling—nervous? Excited? Terrified? I lay there for a few moments working out how I would approach this subject, and to do it in a way that he would believe me. I needed someone to believe me if I were to stop what is about to come. "Okay," I said. "Here goes nothing…"

And then I told him everything…

"What if HP Lovecraft was not telling stories but trying to warn us? What if these creatures he wrote of *actually existed* and are here to bring about our downfall? No, please hear me out! He saw them, he walked among them but if he had come straight out with the truth, he would have been branded crazy and locked up, so he wrote about them in stories with the hope we, the readers, would read between the lines and heed his warnings. What if these creatures got to him in the same way that they got to the characters in his stories, and the way they are coming to get me now? It all started when I came across a book—a collection of all his stories. At first, I too thought of it as nothing more than mere fancy, and I was impressed at how imaginative he was considering the time he wrote his stories. The more I read, the more I began to feel that this man had been ahead of his time, and as I read on, I felt dread forming in the pit of my stomach. To me, these stories started to take on the form of warnings."

"Warnings?"

"Yes. Warnings."

"I dismissed this at first as mere fancy on my part. I would chastise myself for getting so drawn into these works. Out of curiosity, though, I found myself looking further into these creatures, theories, and illustrations based upon his descriptions. I had not realised my spare time was now quickly becoming consumed by these creatures—I had to know more, even though I kept telling myself it was a folly to do so. One evening, whilst browsing the Internet and flicking through HP Lovecraft books I had obtained from the local library, I noticed that Lovecraft had stopped writing for a period of about twelve months. My interest piqued—why? No one can account for his whereabouts during this time, and when he finally returned to writing, it seemed he struggled to put his stories together. I decided I needed to look into that further. Something is not adding up for me, and my instinct is to push it.

"During this period, I had noticed things around me starting to change—like the world I exist in is now very different. It definitely felt different. Colours seemed muted to me and every time I ventured out and about, I found myself looking over my shoulder, unable to let go of this feeling I were being followed. Whilst my existence outside had become dreary, my dreams were the complete opposite—vivid and full of terror. Come night, I would fight falling asleep. I didn't want to be consumed by the terrors that came after me in my dreams—the sounds, the smells, and the fear. I could feel slimy flesh, see the glint of bulbous eyeballs peering from the shadows, the darkness that would hang over me, the cold on my skin. Flashes of white, sharp teeth and jagged, blood-stained claws. I would wake in a sweat, often crying out. Begging with my tormentors to be left alone. One night whilst in the midst of one of these hellish dreams, I saw Lovecraft. Decaying, broken, and frail. He looked right at me, and before he could say anything to me, the darkness consumed him. When I opened my eyes, I could still see the outline of his face against the greying ceiling above my bed—the rising sun slipping her fingers through the cracks of the bedroom curtain, dispelling the horrors of the night before.

"I stayed in my bed that day. I felt exhausted, an ache had crept into my bones. I would leave the comfort of my bed only to use the toilet and to retrieve my laptop and notebook so I could continue my research. I called in sick at work and spent my time searching for meaning to the horrors that were now overtaking my brain. On a whim, I opened up a site and began trawling through uploaded videos—cryptids, paranormal, extra-terrestrial—anything and everything in an attempt to solve this for once and for all, but just like I knew it would, I found myself hurtling down further and further into this hole I had dug for myself when I opened up that cursed book of his stories. There were videos of creatures that resembled the ones he had written about—comments from viewers asking, 'what is this?' and 'this cannot be real…can it?' Crab-like creatures with wings perched above roads, looking at the vehicles passing underneath before stretching out their wings and launching into the sky to the sound of the witnesses screaming and crying out in fear."

"And do you think these creatures are real?"

"Yes. I *know* they are real."

I continued, "The Mi-Go! I watched that clip over and over again. I tried to convince myself it was all fake, but the more I watched it, the more I had to accept that it was indeed real. Videos of people standing at the giant black maws of tombs that had cracked open with the shifting of the earth—cries, howls, and growls seeping out from within the darkness. For those brave or stupid enough to venture in, they captured brief glimpses of glowing eyes, shifting humanoid figures hunched and scurrying up walls or around the corners to avoid the light—spine chilling and unexplainable…except I could explain it—because these wretched creatures come to me every night in my sleep. Video after video, I would watch and link them to all of Lovecraft's stories. They were warnings. Lovecraft had been trying to warn us!

"The next day, following this incredible realisation, the world outside seemed much darker for me. Colder. As I headed out and about running my errands, I noticed people staring at me. Actually, staring at me. Not glancing away in embarrassment, they held my stare and there was a menace to the way they looked at me. I decided to test one and stare back to see if they would break away, only to recoil myself, when its face changed to a grey, pulpy mass with fishlike eyes and a wide mouth. I caught another, staring at me as I collected my train ticket from the vending machine—only this one's face became dark as night, with glowing ember eyes burning into my soul; it opened its mouth to reveal white, sharp, pointed teeth. I swear, Doctor, that this is not from a lack of sleep. I also noticed that everywhere I went that day, the air had been dense with a sickly stench of rot. It was suffocating.

"I found, in the days that followed, these creatures did not feel the need to conceal themselves around me. I could now clearly see these faces of pure horror watching me. Tormenting me. Then they started talking to me—not with their mouths, but talking to me…"

I trailed off…no longer shaking or pressing the palms of my hands into my eyes. Instead, now sweating profusely, I could feel a tension headache coming on due to my eyes being closed tight. I slowly opened my eyes. The light in the office was brighter than I remembered. I squinted and sat up, reaching for the glass of water on the stand next to me. When I regained my focus, I looked at Doctor Meyers who sat patiently in his big armchair, his eyes downcast to the notebook, scribbling down notes. I saw that he was quite a few pages into making notes. I watched as he finished his last sentence, circled something further up on the page, flicked over to a blank sheet and then level his intent gaze at me. I took another swig of the cold water before sitting the glass back down on the side table.

"Please. Continue." Doctor Meyers gestured for me to lie back and pick up where I had left off. "That is, if you feel like you can. I don't want to push you. If at any time it becomes too much, I want you to stop. But, if you are able to do so, I would like to know more about these creatures. You said they were talking to you? How did they talk to you? Do they still talk to you?"

I lay back down, cleared my throat, and gathered my thoughts to continue.

"They talk to me. Not through speaking orally, but with their mind. I can hear them in my mind.

Some only growl or shriek at me. But there are the ones who speak English. They are the ones who terrify me the most, for what they say makes my blood run cold. I can hear them all now. It is a constant cacophony of voices and sounds, warnings, and threats. I am repeatedly told to be prepared for the Great Old One is coming…"

"Who is this Great Old One?" Doctor Meyers interrupts.

"The Great Old One, named Cthulhu, lives in the ocean, where He awaits His time to rise and wipe out life as we know it." I stop and the room is quiet save for the scratching of the pen nib on notepaper.

"Continue," Doctor Meyers says from his side of the room.

I inhale and try to pick out my heartbeat amid the voices that are now starting to rise in excitement; *Yes, yes! Tell him about us! Tell him about the Great Old One. Another convert, another voice to bring the*

Great Old One out from His slumber. TELL HIM MORE!

"Warnings about the end of our world. They watch me all the time because they know what I am doing at any time of the day or night. I am now not sleeping because seeing them walking amongst us during the day and hearing their voices all the time is one thing; but at night when I sleep, they appear with images of violence, death, and destruction. This maddening descent into this hell is going to kill me." I paused to focus on my heartbeat, my mind screaming at the swell of voices to go away. The pen continued to scratch out notes. "A little over a month ago, these statues started appearing. On my doorstep at first. Made of a hard, black stone, they are hideous creatures—bulbous eyes, long claws, and gnashing teeth. The stone is ice cold to the touch, and it feels like it is burning your fingers when you touch it, so you can't hold it for long. To look at them causes dread to take hold in the pit of your stomach and spread. I tried to search up online as to what they were and where they could have come from, but the closest I have come are the descriptions of the statues Lovecraft wrote of in his stories.

"The night following the appearance of the first two statues on my doorstep, I was sitting in the lounge room when a frenzied banging on the window jolted me from my reading. I pulled back the blind and I swear, I swear I saw him. Lovecraft. His pale, sallow flesh hung to his face, tattered and with exposed bone. Flesh missing on his jaw, and without a bottom lip, all he could do was open and close his mouth; his eyes burned wild. He lifted a worm-eaten hand, extending a bony finger to where the two black figures were sitting on my bench next to my laptop. Then a blood-curdling scream escaped from his exposed vocal cords, and then tentacles wrapped around him, snatching him back into the darkness."

"Tentacles?"

"Yes, tentacles. Like an octopus or squid." Silence settled into the room.

"Was this one of your dreams?" asked Doctor Meyers.

"No. No, it wasn't. Like I said, I don't sleep anymore. No, this is all real, as real as you and I are in this room right now. I had flung the window open, overcome by the rancid stench of death mingled with the smell of the ocean. I gagged and called out to the night, but it was dead silent. When I looked over to where the statues were, they were gone. I quickly closed the window and armed myself with a knife and proceeded to search my home for the statues."

"Did you find them?"

"Yes, but they were not in the house."

"Where did you find them?"

"I found them the next day. Out in the backyard. But instead of two statues, there were now seven hideous statues. All made of that black stone. One of the statues, the Great Old One, was held tight though."

"Held tight?"

"Yes."

"What do you mean by that, Angus?"

"It was held tight by a skeletal hand that had been detached from its body."

I open my eyes and look up at the ceiling. I turn my face to Doctor Meyers, and he is now frowning as he scrawls across the pages.

"Please proceed, Angus. What happened next?"

"By this stage I am running on pure fear. Why is this happening to me? Why me? I kept telling myself that this theory I had of heeding Lovecraft's warnings and to be the one who could stop what is coming is nothing more than fancy. I tried to rationalise everything, but it is unravelling; I am unravelling. I left the statues where I had found them in the backyard; I didn't attempt to unclench the skeleton hand from the Great Old One's figurine. The voices were deafening by then and I felt that if I were to stay outside, my head would explode. This constantly being hunted by these creatures is more than I can bear. I went back into my house, and there on the bench sat the seven statues, minus the hand."

"How did that make you feel, Angus? What did you do next?"

A sob escaped my throat as I lay there. "I screamed. I screamed and screamed. The voices were beckoning me to accept our fate, to embrace the coming of the Great Old One. To join them in celebrating our demise. As I screamed, the images from my nightmares flashed up into view—so I am now not safe from this terror in my waking hours."

"What about now, Angus? Are you seeing and hearing these things now?" Without hesitating, I cried out, "Yes! They want you now. They want me to show you what I am seeing because once you do, they can come after you."

"Will you show me?"

"No! No, I won't."

"Do you want to end our session now, Angus?"

I shook my head. I wanted to stay here in this room, to keep talking because it was keeping these monsters at bay. If I were to leave now, they would get me. I had to stay here. "I'm good. I want to keep talking. Please."

"I don't know how long I had been screaming for. I dropped to the floor, pressing the palms of my hands into my eyes to make the images go away. Then, just like that, it all stopped. Complete silence. No voices, no visions. When I stood up, the seven statues were on the bench unmoved. I didn't want to look at them. To do so made me want to vomit. I left my house—I needed to get out of there and get away from those things. I didn't realise that I had left my house still in the clothes I had on from the day before, nor did I worry that I was barefoot. I just needed to walk. I don't know what is worse—the constant bombardment of those voices and the horrors or the silence and normalcy."

"What does that mean?"

"It means, that all of a sudden, everything felt like it did before it had all come crashing into my life. I could go out walking amongst the public and looking at the people as they passed me, and not one of them turned into a hideous creature. The voices were gone; silent. The air now free of that stench. I felt, for the first time in a long time, happiness. I told myself that maybe I had become so overworked, so stressed that this caused this episode to happen. It was all in my head and that now everything would go to go back to normal for me. I stayed out that day. I had walked so far out, I had to catch a bus back across the town to reach my home that evening. All that time with no fear was heavenly."

"How long did you find you had this 'peace'?"

"It lasted for about two, almost three weeks. I went back to normal. I could go back to sleep. I could function again. I got a promotion at work and had just started dating this great woman I had met at a friend's party."

"The statues. What happened to them?"

"I threw them out. That very night I got home from that long walk, I simply put them all in a bag and threw them out in the bin. I didn't even give them a second thought. I didn't want to hold on to them; I didn't want to continue to work out what they were or where they could have come from. I threw them out."

"The feeling of dread and nausea that you mentioned you experienced whenever you looked at these statues—did you not feel that response when you got home?"

"No. Nothing."

"So, tell me then, what happened that has now brought you here, to me, to this facility?"

"My reprieve from the torture ended with the return of the statues. While cleaning out my home office, I found an old, tattered box tucked away in the back corner of the closet. I didn't remember putting anything away up there, so I wrestled it out from behind my books on that shelf and when I opened it, I dropped it in horror—inside it contained the statues and paperwork. Research notes not written in my hand, along with old newspaper clippings covering stories of unexplained encounters and deaths. I recognised these as stories that Lovecraft had written about them in his stories—unusual deaths of those who saw what I am seeing now. At the bottom of all the papers, I found Lovecraft's obituary. My blood ran cold. Suddenly, the box containing the statues and the papers felt very heavy, and I left it on my office desk. The nightmares came back that night too. Lovecraft, decaying, his eyes burning into me. The stench of death and decay mingled with saltwater returned and seemed to coat everything and everyone around me. The creatures were back again, revealing themselves to me, taunting and telling me that I am now trapped and had to embrace my doom. Our doom. In the confines of my home, their voices seeped through the atmosphere and clawed away at my brain again. Constant, incessant babbling, threats, and warnings. *No time left. He is here. No way out.* Over and over again.

"One night I came home from work to find that box sitting in the middle of my lounge room floor. The air thick with that wretched smell—gagging from the stench, I ran about the house, opening all the windows in the hope to clear it. I returned to the old box and sat down next to it, hesitant to open it, but I did. The feeling of fear and nausea immediately tore at me upon seeing the seven statues in the box. I dug underneath them to retrieve the papers and I sat there and went over everything contained in those documents."

I paused to sit up and have another sip of water. I could feel myself starting to tremble again. I sipped the cold water and let it sit in my mouth for a few moments before swallowing. Doctor Meyers set his notebook and pen down on his lap and watched me. His expression was one of concern. He leaned forward, "Angus, do you want to stop now?"

"Do you want me to?"

"I don't want to push you to keep going. I can see that you are visibly distressed, and you have given me enough already to read over and assess. If you want to go back…home, you can. We can pick this up tomorrow?"

I took another sip of water and let it sit there as I thought about it all. The voices quietened down in anticipation of my answer. I didn't want to go "home" yet. I had to finish this because I know my time is fast running out. Underneath my shirt are black tendrils, spreading out just under the surface of my skin. I saw them this morning as the voices chanted "time, time, TIME!" I had to finish this, and I am pinning all my hope on Doctor Meyers being able to do what I have not been able to by way of stopping all of this.

I swallowed the water and resumed my position on the daybed. I clasped my sweating, trembling hands tight over my stomach to try to quell the nerves creating jerking spasms throughout my upper body. The voices began to stir, volume creeping up enough for me to hear them approve of my decision to keep going. As I cleared my throat, I could only hope that I am not condemning another man to his doom.

"I began to read through all the paperwork within that box. I could tell that the papers were old from the discolouring, the tattered edges, and the brittleness. I was mindful of how I handled each piece of paper for fear it would crumble to dust.

"Some of the writing is hard to make out due to being so faded, and there were paragraphs scrawled in a language I do not know. I realised that some were accounts from archaeologists, anthropologists, biologists, doctors, and from Lovecraft himself. What appeared to be more stories, dated during the period he had vanished from writing—apparently, he had stopped writing for a year and people put it down to him being burnt out. As I read the stories before me, I realised he wasn't burnt out—he was investigating. Questioning things around him. He wrote prolifically, and what he wrote of his accounts during this period resembles everything that I have been experiencing myself. With each story, his mental stability appeared to spiral down into sheer terror, despair, and then acceptance of what is to come. In one account, he laments of not being able to speak freely 'the great truth' of what is coming—he knew, even back then, that if he spoke the truth, he would have been certified insane and either locked up or laughed into oblivion. So, he wrote these stories. These creatures are real, the Great Old One is real and is about to rise and when He does, we are all good as gone for the voices tell me all the time that He is merciless and will spare none for what He ultimately desires."

I inhaled and let the breath slowly out from between my slightly parted lips. The breath made a whistling sound as it escaped from me. I realised that Doctor Meyers had stopped writing, and I turned to look at him. He sat there, notebook on his lap, the pen placed across the notebook, and he was staring at me. His eyes were searching me, and I could sense in him a mix of fear and disbelief. "Please…please continue, Angus." He motioned for me to lie back down and continue with my story.

So I did.

"There were photos amongst the papers too. Old photos—black and white and sepia photographs. Some were of the statues in the box next to me on the floor. Some were of people out in the street, from the neck down they were normal, but their faces were distorted—like a blur, as if they had moved their heads really fast. If I looked hard enough, I could make out some familiar faces—bulging black glassy eyes, flat noses, and wide, fishlike mouths. Some were dark as night with glowing lights where the eyes would be. I knew these faces because I see them now. In fact, there is one out in the waiting room when I arrived for this appointment. They are all around us; they walk amongst us, just waiting for the Great Old One to rise. They summon Him with their chants, with their rituals, with the idolisation of these cold, black, ugly statues. They are trying to wake Him up."

"Were there photos of other things too?"

"Yes. Quite a few."

"Such as?"

"There is a sepia photo of a ruined castle that sits upon the precipice of a cliff. It looks like it is barely holding on, but there is a life to it—even in the photo. There are photos of ships, of sailors with a great big mass, of something that they have obviously hauled up from the ocean during their travels. Photos of broken open crypts and gargoyles. Then there are photos of Bedouin Arabs in a desert— a caravan of camels, the guides, and some white men I assume are archaeologists. There are trunks and digging tools and shotguns. In one photo, a white man stands holding a big black book; he looks pleased with his discovery, but the expression on the faces of his guides tells another story; they look upon the book in fear. You can tell from the photo, they do not want to be there."

"Can you see what is on the cover of the book?"

"No. But I would hazard to guess that it is the book that features prominently in Lovecraft's stories—it is the Necronomicon." At the mention of this word, the voices rose in crescendo, deafening me. I immediately put my hands over my ears, but it is of no use—the voices are inside my brain now. "I put the papers and the photos back into the box with the statues. I closed it up and moved it back into my office. I didn't want to be near it. I couldn't sleep that night; the stench returned stronger than ever and as the voices of the creatures taunted me, I found myself cowering on my couch, shaking with fear as they came out from the shadows scratching at my doors and windows. Repeatedly, they tell me I am gone. That I must succumb to Cthulhu. Now I am finding myself almost eager to do so. You know, to accept it. But then I snap out and I fight. I have been fighting so hard." My voice cracked, and I felt hot tears welling up in my eyes.

"Was this what led to the stabbing?"

I nodded and curled up on my side. I tucked my hands up tight under my chin, drawing my knees up towards my chest. My heart began to pump harder in my chest and I believed for a moment that it may very well burst before I could finish what I needed to do.

"Yes. As the night wore on, their attempts to get in escalated. Their shrieks and howls and taunts were all -consuming in my head—my brain felt like it was on fire. As I closed my eyes and covered my ears, I kept talking to myself to make it through the night. At some point, I must have fallen asleep because next thing I knew I am standing on a cliff facing the ocean. In the distance, I could see the ocean bubbling and churning violently and a large dark shape appearing just under the surface. The smell of death was overpowering, and I started vomiting. Screaming from unseen entities tore through my head. Through the black and heavy clouds in the sky, I could make out an iridescent green sky—I had never seen that before—and momentarily distracted, I failed to see the giant form breaking through the ocean's shield.

"It was all I could do to stand there in horror and watch it take shape before my eyes…and then, I am back and sitting on my couch in the light of day. I could still smell death, and I had a smattering of vomit on my shirt and the hems of my pants. Between my toes were blades of grass, and fresh soil covered the soles of my bare feet. But here I am, sitting on my couch like I had been the night before when being attacked by these creatures, before the unseen force snatched me from this realm and planted me in that moment of time."

"You don't suppose that you suffered an episode due to stress, and during the event you had walked outside into your backyard?" Doctor Meyers posited to me.

I shook my head. "No. No. This is real. This happened. This thing had taken to the cliff where I watched the Great Old One awaken. That morning as I sat there on the couch, I realised that the creatures had gone quiet. Outside had gone quiet. The statues were placed in a circle in the middle of the floor, scattered around it were all the papers and photographs. I didn't bring the box out. I swear I never went near it after I had packed away its contents and placed it back in my office. The box had been torn to pieces and scattered amongst the papers that were all over the floor. I also noticed that all the windows in my house were wide open, and on the frames, I could see claw marks. I went through and checked every room, but I was the only one in my house. I can't exactly explain my feelings or thinking at this time. I do remember the quiet because it was deafening. I stepped out of the front door and walked down to the street. At that time of the morning, seven-thirty, there is a burst of activity as my neighbours are busy getting to work, taking their kids to school. It was garbage collection day, but I noticed that none of the neighbours had their bins out. Not a single soul stirred in the street. Not even a sound; you could hear a pin drop. It made the hairs on the back of my neck stand up."

"Hmmmm…" came from over where Doctor Meyers sat. Pen nib scratching on paper—he wrote his notes quickly, keeping pace as my recollections raced on. The skin on my torso began to burn, I knew the black tendrils were spreading out further and squeezing me as I came closer to completing my story. The creatures would occasionally bellow and shrill out in excitement as I inched closer to my own end.

"I went back inside my house and closed the

front door. My television had somehow turned itself on, playing a video clip from You Tube. A research ship, out in the Pacific Ocean, had picked up a sound coming from deep below. In order to hear it, they had slowed down the recording, and this video now taunted me from my television as it ran on a loop. The scientists were trying to determine what and from where this terrifying sound had come from. They, the scientists, had nicknamed it 'The Bloop' and I knew the source of the sound the moment I heard the first play through. With each loop, I felt insanity choking me; my whole body began trembling violently and I could see the ocean, the dark shape underneath taking form and getting closer to the surface. The stench of death filled the room, suffocating me, and the creatures screamed within my head in rapturous chorus 'He is here! The Great Old One is coming now! Cthulhu take us now! He comes for you too. Give in to His will and you will not suffer as much as the nonbelievers!"

"It felt as though my world was closing in on me at that very moment and in that instant, I fled from my house, to get away from that sound and that wretched smell. I ran down my street screaming at the top of my lungs."

"Did you know when you ran from your house, you had a knife in your hand?"

"No."

"Do you remember grabbing the knife before you left your house, Angus?"

"No."

"Do you remember the stabbing?"

"Yes. I do. It was one of His creatures. As I ran, it approached me."

"You mean the man out on his morning jog?"

"What? Yes, I mean no! It was a creature. To anyone else they would have seen a man, but I could see its true form, one of those fishlike beasts coming at me. Smiling at me and chanting, arms outstretched to grab me. I plunged that knife in as hard as I could. I had to. Otherwise, it would kill me!"

I curled up tighter in a ball on the daybed, trying to squeeze myself to stop my panting. My heart now bouncing about in my chest and the creatures began their chanting. Horrid chanting in an alien language.

"The creature dropped. I remember pulling the knife out and running away. I decided I had to take these monsters out on my own. I made my way towards the main part of town where I knew they would be waiting for me."

"Angus, do you remember how many people you stabbed that day?"

"CREATURES. MONSTERS. NOT PEOPLE! I did not stab or kill people. I stabbed and killed creatures. Cthulhu's creatures that had been summoned all those years ago by that archaeologist in the photo who had found that cursed book out in the desert. Creatures that tormented Lovecraft, ultimately taking him over and destroying him, . Now they want me, but I won't let them! I WON'T!"

"Angus, do you remember how many people you stabbed that day?"

I began sobbing; I pushed my face into the cushion.

"You stabbed fifteen innocent people. Eight of them died as a result of your rampage. Angus? Angus, look at me." Doctor Meyers' voice remained steady and gave away no emotion. I shook my head, refusing to look at him. The creatures were overjoyed; *Keep going*, they pushed at me.

"I didn't hurt anyone. These were not humans, I swear! You have to listen to me because I am running out of time now. I need to stop this."

"Angus, I am going to send you home now while I review all of what you have told me. You understand I am to make an assessment now on whether you will be fit to stand trial over this? I will have you taken back to your home now and I will arrange for the nurse to bring in some medication that will help you settle tonight. I know you are scared right now, and you are dealing with something quite unlike I have ever encountered in my entire career. I promise you though that I am here to help you through this. Now, I will let your escort know you are ready to head back now."

With that, he stood up and headed over to the door. He opened it and motioned for the escort—an armed police officer—to come and take me back to my "home." Home for me now is a room on the psychiatric ward. I was in such a frenzied state when arrested, that I could not bear to acknowledge what was happening and where I was being held, so I called it my home—and to help me, I guess the police and Doctor Meyers thought it best to call it home for me too.

The police officer entered the room. I shakily rose to my feet and let him take hold of me by my upper right arm. I could see that he wasn't one of them, and I wouldn't need to hurt him. The officer led me out of the room and into the reception area where the creature had sat, now nowhere to be seen. I felt like my muscles were going to melt off my skeleton—as if I were walking through a hazy dream. With each step, the stench of death grew stronger. The chants slowly rose in volume. The clinking of the keys carried by the ward registrar as he led me back to my "home" sounded awfully loud despite the growing chanting in my brain. The clanging metal sound actually hurt my ears. I winced as we walked, relieved when they opened my door, and I stepped over the threshold into a sterile room containing a bed with a rock-hard mattress. No bedding—as I am considered a "risk"—and there are cameras up in the corners of the ceiling to keep watch as I pace the confines of my room in between my appointments.

The door closed behind me. I heard the clunk of the heavy lock as it slid into place. Silence. The creatures had stopped. I walked slowly over to the bed and sat down on it. I could feel the hard springs underneath the thin film of mattress insulation. I rested my hands in my lap and looked down at my feet. Emotionally, I had been drained. I am fighting a losing battle between sanity and hopelessness. I watched in horror at the black tendrils snaking their way down my arms and into my hands. I could see them spreading out from the hems of my pants and covering my feet. I rubbed my eyes, closing them tight and then opening them in the hopes that this is all nothing more than a nightmare for me to wake from. Each time I tried, the tendrils were still there, the burning under my flesh was excruciating. There was nothing I could do but to wait for the medication to arrive as promised by Doctor Meyers.

I lay down on the hard mattress and stared into the corners of my room, noting that the shadows appeared to be heaving, pulsating. Long arms would stretch out from the dark and from their hands, elongated fingers extended, clawing at the walls and dragging the black mass further out along the walls, the floor, and the ceiling. I didn't move. The voices told me to stay still, and even if I jumped up and ran, where would I go? I am trapped now. Instead, I focus on my breathing, long and deep breaths to fight the terror that is pounding in my chest. I cast my gaze to the door, waiting for the nurse to walk in with my medication. I strained my ears amongst the stirring of cries, growls, screams, murmurs, for the clunk of a door lock being slid open. By now I am so incredibly desperate for that nurse to come in and maybe, just maybe, that would be my chance to escape? I would push her into the room for the shadows to consume, and I would then run for my life. Yes, that would work. I lay and waited and waited in hope for my chance to come. Meanwhile, the shadows were converging and getting closer and closer to my bed. I curled up in a ball, staring at the door and willing for that nurse to walk in.

As I felt the cold slide over me, and as the wretched shadows closed in on me, I heard the door unlock over the creatures' chants. As soon as the door opened, letting light from the hall spill forth and into the room, the shadows pulled back as if in fear. The creatures quickly hushed within my head too, and the figure standing there in the doorway stepped in. I am now crouched on my bed, ready to spring off and to make my break for it. Just as I get ready to take my chance, I realised the figure in my room is not one of the nurses. Though it wore a nurse's uniform, it definitely is not one of the psych ward's nurses. I recoiled in horror. I realise now it is one of the creatures. Its face twisted and hideous. Slime dripped from its wide mouth, curled up at the sides in an evil grin. Its dead eyes bore into mine; its flesh looked like it was going to slide off its skull. In its hands, it held a box. The old box from my house. The box that had been torn to shreds and scattered along with its contents all over my lounge room floor. The box is now intact, and the creature continued to walk towards me with the box.

I fell back onto the bed. I realise there and then that I am not going to get out. Not now, not ever. The creature thrust the box at me and demanded I take it. I didn't want to touch it. I shook my head, I couldn't speak—my vocal cords were frozen. "Take it now. This has to happen. You can't stop it, you fool. The others before you failed us. We are here now, and the Great Old One has risen! All nonbelievers will pay, and we will be rewarded by Cthulhu. He has heard us over time calling for Him, searching the universe for Him. We were woken when man uttered the first line from the Necronomicon. You can't escape now; you are one of us. It won't hurt, I promise."

I looked past the creature to the light coming through the open door. "There will be no leaving this place. Not for you or for anyone else here. This is our place now, your place now. There is no one left who can help you." It stared at me for a while before placing the box on the bed next to me. The creature then turned and headed to the door. It gave me one last look before walking out, closing and locking the door behind it. I suddenly found myself alone again in the room, surrounded by the shadows that began creeping back towards me.

Doctor Meyers sat slumped over his desk. The notes from the session with Angus Ford were set out in front of him, a thick dark crimson fluid seeped out and over the notes, and across the desk. The colour drained from Doctor Meyers' body, escaping through the large gash in his neck. The cut is so deep, his head was held on by a few tendons and skin. The nurse had materialised as if from the air, and no sooner had he realised, he had no time to react to the swift and precise attack. He heard the flesh and sinew of his neck being cleaved open and then it was all over. Slumped over the desk, bleeding out over the notes in his office with no one aware of what had just taken place, the silence would occupy the room until the discovery of his body the next morning by his receptionist.

With the shadows getting closer, I reached for the box. The moment I laid my hand on it, the shadows stopped moving—they appeared to freeze in anticipation. The creatures whispered at me to open the box, "Join us now before we change our minds! You found us and now we must close the circle to complete our task, for Cthulhu awaits and

He is not a patient God." I proceeded to open the box, expecting to find the statues and the paperwork. I am surprised to find a dark grey robe along with the seven ugly statues. Underneath the robe and statues, my fingertips brushed a soft, textured surface. I removed the robe and the statues to reveal a large and very old-looking book. I knew what it was. The Necronomicon. I lifted it out from the box and set it down in my lap. I stared at it for a while before taking the cover up with my fingertips, opening it. "STOP! DO NOT OPEN IT JUST YET!" the creatures screamed, piercing my ears; causing me incredible pain. "First you must prepare. The robe."

I put the book down on the bed and picked up the grey robe. Made of a thick woollen fabric, the robe reeked of that familiar death stench. I recoiled, vomit rising up in my throat. My brain begging me not to do it, but I felt as though I were now in a trance as I slipped the robe over my head and pulled it down over my body, setting it in place with the sash around my waist. I couldn't stop myself, I felt as if I had no control of my physical form. "Now the statues of our Elder Gods, you need to set them out in a circle." My body willingly moved about the room, setting the statues up as instructed by the creatures, while my brain continued to plead with me to stop. The creatures were excited now. With the statues now in place, I returned to my bed. I sat down again and looked over my room. The shadows were pulsating, inching out towards the circle of Gods. In the corner of the room, from out of the shadows, a form was taking shape. It was him! It was Lovecraft! This time he wasn't decaying like he had been on previous visits. He appeared perfectly normal, fully formed. He remained within the boundary of the shadows cast on the floor as he looked at me and began speaking:

"Finally, after all this time, we have found another who can see into this realm! You were able to see what I saw and now you are the one to complete it for us."

"What, what do you mean *us*?" I stammered. "You were trying to warn me, trying to tell me how to end this!"

"No. Not end, but to begin. You see, all my research was to make this happen, but unfortunately, I did not live long enough to complete the task for Cthulhu. I have languished for an eternity, waiting for another with the sight to come along. Here you are! Don't be afraid. This needs to happen. Humanity needs this to happen, for we are spiralling out of control and Cthulhu is the one to make it right again. To obliterate Earth and start anew."

My body began to tense up, and a hot prickling sensation ran over my skin. "I won't do it! If you are saying that this is going to wipe out life, I won't do it! I can't and I won't!" Lovecraft stepped forward within the shadow boundary, shaking his head. "I am afraid you now don't have a choice. It has to be finished, or we finish you." His face grew dark, his eyes burned bright, and his smile revealed sharp, pointed teeth. I drew back on my bed, pushed up against the wall to get as far away from him as I could. The shadows began moving forward, and so too did Lovecraft. "Join us." He reached out his hand, and as it passed through the shadow, his flesh disappeared, revealing a skeletal hand. He wriggled his fingers, hand palm up, inching closer and closer to me.

The room is now bitingly cold. I continue to fight back the fear that is crushing me and I keep looking at the door praying for that nurse to come in with the medication and this would all just go away with a pill. My brain was misfiring and as a result I am pulled deep into this other world of horror and turmoil. This could not be real. "Oh, but it is so very real! Join us, Angus, and help us achieve the greatest thing ever and we will stand by Cthulhu's side as He reigns over the universe. We have waited so long now. Do not disappoint us, Angus!" His voice rolled into a sinister growl as he spoke. Everything I had known of this life is now being obliterated right here and now in this room. My options were limited to say the least and I am now backed into a corner with shadows converging upon Lovecraft and I—me, trying to resist, and he, pushing me to destruction.

In my head I can hear the creatures chanting, and the Necronomicon next to me began to thrum along with it. The gold lettering embossed on the leather cover—a leather cover made of human skin—is now glowing, and I swear I can hear the ocean in the room. A heavy force is pressing on me, my bones feel like they are about to splinter into dust, and there stands Lovecraft, eyes burning bright, watching and waiting for me to choose my next move. The air in the room is starting to thin; I begin to gasp, and my head feels like it is detached from my body. I start laughing at the book on the bed, which is now suspended in the air. The cover glowing, vibrating with the chanting that is growing louder by the minute. I can feel my blood coursing through my body. The ocean roars now and there is a creaking emanating from the corners of the room. The shadows have settled upon my shoulders and I know I am done. I have to make a decision now. The stench of death and salt from the ocean is overpowering, and I wretch and heave as I take hold of the book and stand up, leaving the bed.

I give one last look at the door of my room, desperately holding out for hope that I would be saved, and I would not have this burden to carry. I didn't want this. I didn't ask for this; it found me. They found me through his stories, stories that I thought were warnings but were instead their guide to find the next link in their chain, the one to bring them to Cthulhu and the one to bring destruction to life as we know it. The Necronomicon is cold and heavy in my hands as I slowly walk across the room to take my place within the Elder Gods' Circle. As I step over the invisible threshold and into the circle, it lights up with an iridescent green light—the same green as the light I saw in the sky when standing on the precipice overlooking the ocean. The creatures' voices grow thick and deep as the chanting intensifies, becoming a frenzy in anticipation of what they have waited for so long for.

Lovecraft stands by the circle staring at me, urging me towards my destiny. "Be our saviour! You will be rewarded, we will overlook the deaths of our kin at your hands. You will be forgiven and celebrated; we and the universe need this NOW! Don't be scared, you do this, and everything will be right. Don't do this and we will make you suffer for eternity." As I approach the centre of the circle, I notice my feet and the hem of my robe are wet. I look down to see the floor is now covered with water that laps at my ankles with every step I take. I feel like my body is not my own, not within my control, but my mind is still fighting, and I have to see this through now. No one is going to save me from this, but maybe I can save them.

I stand in the centre of Gods' Circle, bringing the Necronomicon up from my side, holding it out in front of me. My brain is pushing to make one final attempt of control as I open the book to the page as directed by Lovecraft. "Just read out the paragraph, wake Him up and let Him carry out His destiny as you stand here now carrying out yours." My eyes scan the page before me, a language I had never seen before, but I understood it clearly—*Ph'nglui mglw'nafh Cthulhu R'lyeh wgah'nagl fhtagn.*

"Read it out!" Lovecraft cried out over the now deafening chanting of the creatures. The shadow has consumed the whole room now and is pulsating with the intense energy that is surrounding me and this book. The circle glows, and beneath my feet, a green orb lights up. It casts an eerie glow about us, and I can make out the limbs and deformed heads bobbing within the dark mass surrounding me.

I am ready. I have to do this now. As I draw in my final breath, the chanting stopped, and all is quiet. I look at the words on the page, my brain regaining control in that moment of silence. I steady my hands, firming up my grip on the cover, feeling the human leather sends a cold chill down my spine. Lovecraft is frozen in anticipation, I watch his expression of elation of seeing his dream become a reality turn to pure rage and disbelief as I shut the Necronomicon and drop it, hearing it splash. The green light dies out, Lovecraft screams in rage and rushes toward me digging his fingers into my face, he forces me down under the water, and then…there is nothing.

The nurse hurried from the dispensary across the ward. She had just filled the script for their new patient, Angus Ford, at the order of Doctor Meyers, but she had been side-tracked when another nurse asked her to help her with a schizophrenic patient on the other side of the hospital wing. The nurse quickened her pace as Angus Ford should have had his medication over an hour ago. She approached the registrar's desk and informed him she was there to administer treatment to the patient. The registrar signed her in, then led her down the long corridor to the last room on the ward.

Taking the keys from his belt, the registrar found the room key, and inserted it into the lock. A heavy clunk sound signalled the door unlocking, and he pulled the handle, opening the door. The nurse and registrar stepped into the room and were shocked at what they found. In the centre of the room a wet, crumpled up grey robe lay on the floor. The room was empty save for the bed and the robe. The nurse immediately ran out into the hall and hit the alert button. The alarm blared through the ward, and security and medical staff rushed to the location. All were at a loss as to where Angus could have gone to. The room's camera turned out to be faulty, despite being given all clear during a maintenance check a few days earlier. The hospital now placed on lockdown as police were called in to search for the missing patient. The following morning, Doctor Meyers' receptionist found his body at his desk—the theory then was that Angus had escaped, killing Doctor Meyers before fleeing the hospital.

No one knew how close they had come to being completely wiped out by a brutal alien *God*. Angus saved humanity that night, and now *they* must wait for another link to come along.

ABOUT THE AUTHOR

JAMSINE JARVIS is an Australian author of Speculative Fiction. After joining a local writing group in May 2019, she was encouraged to try her hand at writing fiction - sending off her first pieces of fiction into **Black Hare Press'** call out for *Beyond*. Realising how much fun this writing gig is, and how much she loves to tell stories, Jasmine has continued to shape her writing and is drawn to the absurd, the creepy and the downright terrifying. Since landing her spot in *Beyond*, she has had 23 drabbles and 4 short stories published. Jasmine hopes her readers enjoy her stories as much as she enjoys writing them.

Bibliography

Ancients, Black Hare Press, 2020

Apocalypse, Black Hare Press, 2019

Bad Romance, Black Hare Press, 2020

Beyond, Black Hare Press, 2019

Lockdown: Horror, Black Hare Press, 2020

Love, Black Hare Press, 2020

Oceans, Black Hare Press, 2020

Sideshow Alley, Little Quail Press, 2019

The Rise of the Great Old One, Black Hare Press, 2020

Unravel, Black Hare Press, 2019

Connect

Twitter: @jjarvisauthor

Instagram: jasmine_jarvis_author_

Amazon: amazon.com/Jasmine-Jarvis/e/B07XZ8G9J8

ABOUT THE PUBLISHER

BLACK HARE PRESS is a small, independent publisher based in Melbourne, Australia.

Founded in 2018, our aim has always been to champion emerging authors from all around the globe and offer opportunities for them to participate in speculative fiction and horror short story anthologies.

Connect

Website: *www.blackharepress.com*

Twitter: *@BlackHarePress*

74

75

81

83

84

THE RISE OF THE GREAT OLD ONE

85

87

9 781925 809794